Praise for
A Wolf at the G

"*A Wolf at the Gate* is a simple story that evokes profound and fundamental themes: survival, hunger, war and violence, law and justice, fear, greed, and predation. In the hands of Mark Van Steenwyk it becomes a transformative parable of truth and reconciliation, the power of community, and the dazzling force of love enacted in the public square, the very heart of justice."
> —Bill Ayers, author of *Public Enemy: Confessions of an American Dissident*

"Van Steenwyk retells the story of St. Francis of Assisi [with] a clever shift that adds tension and new beauty to a familiar tale. . . . As a result of her instruction from the Beggar King, Sister Wolf comes to understand that all life is worth preserving and that loving kindness is the greatest of all gifts. Influenced by Japanese woodblock prints, Hedstrom's stark, solid, and lovely illustrations appear throughout."
> —*Publishers Weekly*

"Van Steenwyk writes in sharp, muscular prose highly suitable for the fabulistic subject matter, deftly navigating both the darker and lighter segments of the story. The true standouts of the book, however, are the illustrations by Joel Hedstrom . . . full-page illustrations in brilliant colors that feel simultaneously ancient and stylishly contemporary. The result is a book out of time: a coupling of narrative and illustration that should stoke the imagination of any young modern reader."
> —*Kirkus* (starred review)

"A profound and beautiful work, I pray that it will be widely read and shared with children and adults alike."
> —*Englewood Review of Books*

"What a cutting-edge book! This retelling of a timeless story through fresh eyes not only provides a deeper insight into its original values, it also gives the story contemporary relevance. And the illustrations are an absolutely perfect embodiment of the book's soul."
    —Innosanto Nagara, author of *A Is for Activist*

"In a tale akin to a parable, *A Wolf at the Gate* presents a simple story that opens up the heart and mind to the profound truths of peace, love and compassion. A timely book for all ages."
    —Jamie Arpin-Ricci, author of *The Cost of Community: Jesus, St. Francis, and Life in the Kingdom*

"Adventures and travels blend with accounts of little acts of kindness and courage to create a compelling fable that all ages will enjoy in a story of promises and hard lessons learned in the forest of life."
    —Diane Donovan, *Midwest Book Review*

"This timely fable will make young and old alike question the way we live and the way we react to challenges."
    —Duncan Tonatiuh, author of *Pancho Rabbit and the Coyote: A Migrant's Tale*

"In *A Wolf at the Gate*, we find a medieval fable made potently relevant. With solid prose and timeless illustrations, this book is recommended to all families passionate about social justice and living in harmony with the earth."
    —Chris Crass, author of *Towards Collective Liberation: Anti-Racist Organizing, Feminist Praxis, and Movement Building Strategy*

"In his wonder-filled reimagining of the legend of Saint Francis and the wolf, Mark Van Steenwyk weaves a twisting, spellbinding, always-surprising tale of fear and redemption and, ultimately, peace."
    —Arthur Salm, author of *Anyway**

A WOLF AT THE GATE

A WOLF AT THE GATE

Mark Van Steenwyk

Illustrated by Joel Hedstrom

PM Press
PO Box 23912
Oakland, CA 94623
www.pmpress.org

Reach & Teach
144 W. 25th Avenue
San Mateo, CA 94403
www.reachandteach.com

ISBN: 978-1-62963-150-9
Library of Congress Control Number: 2016930962

10 9 8 7 6 5 4 3 2 1

Printed in the USA by the Employee Owners of Thomson-Shore in Dexter, Michigan.
www.thomsonshore.com

For Jonas.

"Lord, make me an instrument of thy peace.

Where there is hatred, let me sow love."

— SAINT FRANCIS OF ASSISI

Contents

1

Lords of the Forest

This story begins with the birth of a wolf.

She was born under the red glow of the Hunter's Moon. She was a strange pup; her fur was blood red. None of the wolves in the pack had ever seen a wolf with such red fur. Her mother and father knew that she was destined for important things.

They slept in a small cave whose opening was hidden by the sweeping branches of a fir tree. Beast and bird proclaimed her birth throughout the forest, for the wolves ruled the forest. And this pup's parents ruled the wolf pack.

In those days, when a royal pup was born, a holy month was declared. All were safe from the wolves' tooth and claw. For an entire month, the beasts of the forest came to honor the little red wolf—the

creeping things like snakes and frogs, the soaring things like bats and birds, and the running things like deer and foxes.

From every family of beast, all came to celebrate the birth of the red wolf.

The wolf father taught her all the wisdom passed down from his own parents. He taught her how to hunt deer near the edge of the forest, where the river meets the tall grass. He taught her how to fight as they wrestled together in the golden warmth of the setting sun. Most importantly, he taught his daughter how to hide from their greatest enemy, humankind, by sticking to the shadows, since wolves can see better in the dark.

The wolf father also taught the red wolf legends passed down from pack to pack since wolves first hunted in the mountains they called home.

One night, as the sky grew dark and the crickets began their nightly chorus, the red wolf and her father stood at the top of a small mountain. Looking down upon the village of Stonebriar at the foot of the mountain, the wolf father snarled and told her of the wolves' first clash with humankind:

* * *

Once, there was no village below . . . no walls of stone or houses of wood. No humans with their weapons of steel and iron. No plowed fields, no row upon row of wheat. No humans building fences to enslave wild things. The forest was in balance. The streams teemed with trout. The trees chimed with birdsong. Deer danced through the fields. There was enough food for the pack, and our pack was large.

We were the Lords of the Forest.

Then the humans came.

I tell you this story as my father told it to me. And now I tell it to you. Listen, and remember.

At first, the ancient wolves lived at peace with the humans. But food became scarce. The humans uprooted the trees and planted fields. They tore stones from the earth and built walls. And they began to hunt the wolves, so they could have the deer and rabbits for themselves. Their fields and villages grew as the forest shrank.

Desperate and hungry, the ancient wolves fought back. But the humans' metal claws reach farther than ours. Their metal teeth cut deeper than our teeth of bone. In the first battle between wolves and humans, many wolves died. Only a few survived.

Humans don't just kill to survive. Sometimes, they kill out of rage. And they don't just eat to survive; sometimes, they eat when their belly is already full. They are violent and greedy. They aren't like any of the other beasts in the forest; they want to own it all.

That is why we, the Lords of the Forest, hide deep in the shadows and high in the mountains. We wait and watch. We live in fear.

*   *   *

Early one morning, the wolf mother caught the red wolf eating more than her share of food.

The wolf mother looked at her daughter with sad eyes and said, "Let's go for a walk."

As the orange oak leaves basked in warm light of the sun, the red wolf and her mother walked along the path to the river. They listened as the cawing of the ravens joined the bubbling laughter of a nearby stream. A chittering squirrel ran across their path. As they stopped to listen, the wolf mother told this tale:

*   *   *

There once was a raven. He was clever, but lazy. Every day, he perched in the upper branches of the tallest tree in the forest to watch the animals rushing about, storing food for the coming winter. Of all the creatures of the forest, one squirrel worked hardest. She gathered food from sunrise to sunset.

Raven wanted all those nuts for himself. Instead of working hard like Squirrel to lay aside food for the coming winter, he simply waited for Squirrel to go out searching for nuts. While she was out, Raven

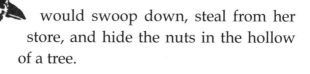

would swoop down, steal from her store, and hide the nuts in the hollow of a tree.

Squirrel noticed that, no matter how hard she worked, her store of nuts grew smaller, not larger.

One day, Squirrel came home to find her store completely empty. She suspected that Raven was the thief but had no proof. Discouraged, she moved to another part of the forest to start over.

Next, Raven watched a jay gather and bury acorns. While Jay was out, Raven would dig up his acorns, making sure to cover the hole again, and hide them in the hollow of a tree.

Jay noticed that, no matter how hard he worked, his store of acorns was growing smaller, not larger. One day, Jay came home to find his stash of acorns completely empty. Jay suspected Raven had stolen from him but had no proof. Discouraged, Jay moved to another part of the forest to start over.

Raven continued his tricksy ways with the other animals below. In the end, Raven was all alone; his neighbors had moved to other parts of the forest in search of food.

Raven said to himself, "I don't mind! I'd rather be well-fed and lonely than hungry with neighbors!"

One day, while Raven was in his tree hollow eating like a king, a terrible storm blew through the forest. Lightning struck the tree, setting it aflame. The Raven was able to fly to safety, but all of his ill-gotten food burned to ash.

He flew throughout the forest. Finding Squirrel's new home, he begged, "Squirrel, I am hungry, share your food with me!"

Squirrel replied, "Go away! I have little enough for myself and can't trust you."

Raven flew away, sad. Next, he found Jay's new home. He said, "Jay, I am hungry, share your food with me!"

Angry, Jay yelled, "Leave me alone! I have little enough for myself and can't trust you."

Raven flew throughout the forest in search of his old neighbors. Each time they responded the same way. Alone and hungry, Raven flew away; none of the other animals ever saw him again.

*　*　*

The wolf mother looked into her daughter's eyes and said, "It is better to be hungry with neighbors than to be well-fed alone."

The wolf mother and father continued to share wisdom with their daughter as she grew.

Seasons passed. The wolf father and mother grew old and died. After a time of mourning, the red wolf became the unchallenged chief of her pack.

At first, she led her pack wisely. She was respected for her hunting skills and her ability to keep the pack safe from the humans. Every night, under the pale glow of the moon, she taught her pack all the tales of their wolf ancestors.

No amount of wisdom, however, could keep the humans who lived in the valley below from hunting more and more deer and rabbits. There wasn't enough food for the wolves. Some of the weaker wolves died of hunger.

The red wolf's wisdom began to give way to rage. She hated the human beings for what they had done to wolfkind throughout generations. Desperately, foolishly, she believed the pack could drive the humans from the land.

Most of the pack wanted to leave the forest in search of a new home, but the red wolf stubbornly refused. "Since ancient times, this has been our forest. We were here long before the humans came. We will never leave," she said, day after day.

As food grew scarcer, the pack grew angrier. They blamed the red wolf for their troubles. So it was that another wolf in the pack challenged her leadership; the winner of a fight would be the chief.

The red wolf was faster and stronger and fiercer. The two wolves slashed at each other with their claws and snapped at each other with their teeth. The red wolf kept the upper paw . . . until she stumbled over the twisted root of an old oak tree. Seizing the moment, the challenger attacked, brutally gnawing on the red wolf's hind leg. The red wolf had been defeated.

Following their new chief, the pack left, leaving the red wolf bleeding in the shadow of that oak tree. Both her leg and her heart stung with pain.

She never saw any of them again.

Slowly, painfully, she limped into a nearby cave . . . the cave where she had been born.

The red wolf was now the last wolf in the forest.

2

The Blood Wolf

Without a pack, the red wolf hunted alone. With a wounded leg, she was too slow to catch most prey; everything from the gracefully loping deer to the scurry-footed squirrels were too quick to catch.

For a few days, the red wolf was able to fill her belly with wild berries and mice. But winter was near. Berry bushes would sleep for the winter and mice would find refuge under the snow. When that happened, the red wolf would die of hunger.

She had one chance. Humans kept animals in barns and fences. They were easy prey. Although sheep and cows and chickens are delicious, they are a risky meal. The clever humans set traps with iron jaws and shoot arrows with iron tips. Through such tools of violence, humans kill wolves from afar.

As the days passed, the red wolf's fear lessened as her hunger grew.

Late one night in early autumn, when thick clouds covered the moon, the red wolf sneaked onto a farm at the edge of the village of Stonebriar. Following the scent of chickens carried in the cool air, she slid under a heavy wooden fence and made her way to the chicken coop. The door to the coop was latched shut. This would have been a challenge to a duller creature, but the red wolf easily pulled the wooden latch open with her teeth.

The chickens, of course, weren't happy to find a wolf in their coop. They clucked in terror as the red wolf seized one of the hens and hobbled off to her cave in the cover of darkness. That night, she ate better than she had in months . . . even better than before her pack abandoned her, since she didn't have to share her meal with anyone else.

The red wolf slept well with a belly filled with meat and a soul filled with revenge; it felt good to take food from the humans.

The next night, the red wolf sneaked onto the farm again. As the nights continued, she grew bolder. Soon, chickens weren't enough; her mouth watered as she imagined cat or lamb or beef for dinner.

The farmers set traps, of course, but the red wolf carefully avoided them. The traps were poorly hidden and stunk of human. They must have thought she was a dumb beast, rather than a Lord of the Forest!

Her rage grew with her hunger. Since the days of the ancient wolves, humans had only brought death and slavery. Now, she was the last wolf in the forest. She needed to teach the humans to fear her teeth and claws more than she feared their iron weapons.

She began to feast earlier and earlier in the day. Soon, she was walking onto farms in broad daylight. She ate whenever she felt like it. She grew stronger and angrier with each passing day. Her hind leg no longer hurt, though she wasn't as fast as she once was.

The farmers tried to shoot her with arrows, of course. But wolf senses are much better than human senses. The red wolf's ears heard even the smallest shifting of leaves under human feet. Her eyes caught the quick motion of human hands reaching for arrows. By the time an arrow sprung from the bow, the red wolf had already stepped aside.

News spread of a clever red wolf who evaded the arrows and traps of farmers. Anxiously, the village sent two brave hunters to slay the troublesome wolf.

Nobody saw the hunters again.

The village sent a few soldiers. They never returned. Fear gripped the people.

News spread; as families gathered around the fireplace, they told stories of the "blood wolf" who not only outwitted farmers but murdered hunters. As fear rooted in the hearts of the people of Stonebriar, the tales grew wilder.

Some said the Blood Wolf was as large as a cow with teeth as long as daggers. Others said the wolf wasn't a wolf at all but a demon that escaped from hell. Some said that the Blood Wolf ate disobedient children. None of these, of course, were true. People tell strange stories when they are afraid.

The people wouldn't leave the village, night or day. Few ventured outside their homes, fearing the Blood Wolf. At night, when the red wolf howled at the moon, old men and women would faint with fear. Children would pull their blankets over their heads. Even the bravest of men and women would shiver with dread.

3

King of the Beggars

Stonebriar was under siege.

In those days, a beggar came to the village. He wore a simple brown robe and his feet were bare. The people of Stonebriar called him "the Beggar King."

The Beggar King was beloved by the common folk, for he was a generous and loving man. Wherever he went, he shared whatever he had: a loaf of bread, a happy song, a kind word. Even the rich treated him with respect. The people of Stonebriar, especially the poor, loved visits from this holy man.

The Beggar King was a friend to all creatures. Most animals of the forest feared humans, but when the Beggar King walked through the forest, birds would land on his shoulder and offer a joyful song. Rabbits and squirrels would run near his feet in hopes of getting a scrap of bread.

The Beggar King heard rumors about the Blood Wolf that threatened the peace of Stonebriar. He felt compassion for the people.

Appearing before the council of village leaders, the Beggar King offered to help save Stonebriar from the savage jaws of the Blood Wolf.

"If you look for that evil wolf, you won't come back!" they proclaimed.

The Beggar King wouldn't change his mind, no matter how loudly the village council argued. He simply said: "If you leave out any of God's creatures from the shelter of compassion and pity, you will treat one another the same way."

The council gave in. They knew in their hearts that the Beggar King would become wolf food.

The Beggar King made his way to the cave where the Blood Wolf was rumored to live.

Suddenly, the wolf rushed out of the cave, snarling. A low growl rumbled in her throat. The Beggar King offered up a simple prayer, thinking he might die. At that moment, the wolf stopped short, baring its teeth.

The Beggar King stood, motionless, as he looked the red wolf in the eyes. This surprised the wolf, who was used to humans running away or falling to the ground in fear. Occasionally, bolder humans—like hunters or soldiers—would lunge at her with a cry of rage. This man, however, stood still.

There was something else strange about this man: the way he smelled. Every creature had its own smell. Rabbits smelled of thistle and burdock and soil. Deer smelled of coneflower and rye. Humans had the strangest smell. They rubbed their hands in all manner of strange things. No two humans smelled the same, but they had smells in common: iron, wheat, fire, and, underneath it all, the sickly sweet tang of fear.

This man smelled of wheat and fire, but there was no smell of iron or fear. In its place were the scents of the forest: willow and pine, raven and stone.

The snarl fell from the red wolf's mouth. She tilted her head to the side and stared into the eyes of the strange man who didn't smell like a man.

They stood looking into each other's eyes for several moments before the man spoke. "Sister Wolf," he said, with a voice quivering more from sadness than fear, "you have made enemies of the people of Stonebriar, who curse you for your murderous hunger."

As she stared into the man's eyes, the wolf noticed another strange thing. She saw in his eyes the same look her mother had given her when she, as a young pup, had done something wrong (like taking food that didn't belong to her).

The Beggar King's eyes shone with the same mix of sadness and love. Here stood her ancient enemy, and this enemy was looking at her with her mother's eyes.

There was yet another strange thing about this man. When sneaking near the dens where the humans slept, the wolf had heard them speak. To the red wolf's ears, human speech sounded like the whimpering of newborn wolf pups . . . meaningless and clumsy. This man, however, spoke slowly in a language she could understand.

Slowly, he said to her, "Sister Wolf, you are a creature of the forest, but have become like a human. You kill out of rage. You eat when your belly is already full. You are violent and greedy, like those you hate."

The red wolf hung her head in shame. The strange man was right: she was no longer acting like a wolf, but a human.

The man continued: "I will make peace between you and Stonebriar, Sister Wolf. Stop hurting these people and their animals and you will be forgiven."

At this, the red wolf walked up to the Beggar King, and sat at his feet. The Beggar King bent low and extended his hand. The wolf had once seen two humans in the village greet each other by grasping each other's hands, so she carefully placed her paw into the Beggar King's outstretched hand.

The wolf no longer felt lonely; she now had a friend.

The Beggar King smiled. "Since you are willing to make peace, I promise you that you will be fed every day by the people of Stonebriar as long as you remain at peace with them. You will no longer be hungry, since it was hunger that drove you to such violence. And you must never harm them . . . do you agree?"

The red wolf yipped in agreement. The Beggar King smiled.

Growing serious, he said, "The people of Stonebriar are afraid. They need a friend like you, Sister Wolf. They have forgotten how to enjoy the sunshine and the rain, the wildflowers of the fields and birds of the air. Will you watch over these good people as a mother or father watches over their babies?"

The red wolf yelped in affirmation.

The Beggar King laughed, "The people of Stonebriar are your pack now! Come with me, Sister Wolf."

The red wolf followed the Beggar King as he walked back to Stonebriar.

4

Sister Wolf

Two guards stood watch at the city gate.

In the distance, they saw the Blood Wolf approach. They didn't see the Beggar King at first for he was dressed all in brown and blended into the color of the dusty road.

Their eyes opened wide in fear. One guard's hand shook so violently that he dropped his bow and screamed like a scared child.

The other guard remained calm. He had been a guard for many, many years. His beard was grey, and his hands were steady. Still, his heart raced as he bellowed: "There's a wolf at the gate!"

As the grey-bearded guard nocked his arrow, he spotted the Beggar King.

"Hold your arrows!" shouted the Beggar King. "This wolf comes in peace!"

The other guard (who had since stopped screaming) ran all the way to the far side of the village to tell the council of the Blood Wolf's arrival.

By the time all of the members of the council had reached the city gate, a crowd of townsfolk had gathered, bubbling with chatter. A dozen guards accompanied the council.

Calling the city guards to ready their spears, the mayor, who was the leader of the council, commanded: "Open the gate!"

The grey-bearded guard silently obeyed. Slowly, he raised the gate.

The red wolf ambled through the gate, the Beggar King at her side. She stopped a few paces from the mayor. The Beggar King rested his hand upon her head and stroked her soft, furry ears.

Upon seeing the Blood Wolf behaving more like a pet dog than a wild wolf, the people fell silent.

The Beggar King broke the silence: "This wolf has promised never to harm you again—neither you, nor any of your livestock."

At this, the people of Stonebriar stood silent. They were confused, yet filled with hope for the first time in many days.

"However," the Beggar King continued, "I have promised that you, the people of Stonebriar, will feed her when she is hungry. For it is hunger that drove her to violence. Will you honor my promise?"

Huddling together, the council discussed the matter. After whispering for a few minutes, the mayor declared: "As the leader of Stonebriar, I promise that we will feed the Blood Wolf so long as she remains a peaceful wolf."

Smiling, the Beggar King said, "Then you must call her 'Blood Wolf' no longer." Patting the red wolf on the head, he declared: "From now on, we must call her 'Sister Wolf!'"

The people cheered.

Sister Wolf walked up to the mayor, sat upright at his feet, and extended a paw. Confused, the mayor reached out his trembling hand and took her paw. The deal was struck!

* * *

The Beggar King stayed in Stonebriar for several weeks to help Sister Wolf settle into her new way of life.

Sister Wolf felt uncomfortable going door to door for food like a stray dog. And the people of the town were still afraid of welcoming a wolf to their doorstep.

And so, at daybreak, the Beggar King would meet Sister Wolf at the mouth of her cave. The two friends would walk into town, knock on a villager's door, and ask for breakfast. After breakfast, the Beggar King and Sister Wolf would go for a walk along the countryside until the afternoon.

Then they would visit the next house in Stonebriar and ask for supper.

During their countryside walks, Sister Wolf taught the Beggar King wolf-speech and the Beggar King taught Sister Wolf about humankind.

Sister Wolf asked, "Beggar King, why do some families live in big houses while others live in small houses? Some even make houses for chickens and dogs. Yet many beg and have no homes at all?"

The Beggar King wasn't sure how to answer. They walked together silently for a time. He looked up at the turtledoves, resting up in the trees, their cozy nests looked the same. Among the birds, there weren't beggars and lords.

Eventually, he said, "Some people have big houses because they want to impress the people with

smaller houses. And some folks have no houses because nobody will share their house with them."

Stunned, Sister Wolf yowled: "That makes no sense!"

The Beggar King agreed.

Sister Wolf asked, "Beggar King, why do some people eat big meals while others eat small meals . . . and still others rarely eat anything at all? The cows and pigs eat far better than many of the beggars on the street!"

Again, the Beggar King didn't know how to answer. He walked alongside his four-legged friend in silence for quite some time. He looked at some frogs jumping and splashing at the pond nearby. There weren't fat frogs and starving frogs. They all ate what they needed and no more; there was plenty for all.

A while later, he said, "Some people eat big meals because their hearts are empty. Some people eat humble meals because their hearts are content. And some others eat too little because nobody will share their food with them."

Shocked, Sister Wolf growled, "That's horrible!"

The Beggar King agreed.

* * *

In time, the Beggar King bade Sister Wolf farewell so that he could visit friends and strangers in another town. By then, the townsfolk had grown comfortable with the sight of Sister Wolf.

When villagers heard scratching at their door, followed by a happy bark, they knew that Sister Wolf had come to ask for food. Some were generous, others less so. But Sister Wolf never took more than she needed, though sometimes she took extra to share with those who had too little to eat.

Many grew to love Sister Wolf. Some parents let their children play with her. When she was in a good mood, she'd let smaller children ride upon her back. Some of the naughtiest children would pull her fur too hard. Even then, Sister Wolf wouldn't growl but simply remember the scent of that child and never let them ride on her back again.

So great was the change in Sister Wolf that she went to the farm animals and promised to never harm them again. They were much slower to trust Sister Wolf than the humans had been. At first, one sight of Sister Wolf terrified them. But in time, they too learned to love her.

Well, that's not entirely true. There was one rooster named Grumpus who never trusted Sister Wolf. After all, she had eaten some of his cousins during one of her nighttime chicken raids. Whenever the wolf came near his farm, he'd flap to the top of the chicken coop and crow loudly: "Kiki-riki . . . flee, flee, flee!"

None of the other farm animals paid any attention to Grumpus, but Sister Wolf felt sad. She did her best to apologize; she'd leave scraps of bread by the chicken coop. But Grumpus never forgave her.

For months, the villagers knew when Sister Wolf was visiting the farm near the west end of the village; they could hear the loud piercing crow of Grumpus: "Kiki-riki . . . flee, flee, flee!"

5

The Outlaws Attack

Sister Wolf missed her old pack but was content with her new pack: the village of Stonebriar.

She loved many of the villagers like family. Especially the children. Whenever Sister Wolf felt lonely, the bright laughter of children would drive away the fog in her heart.

Nevertheless, there were things about Stonebriar that troubled Sister Wolf.

The nobility and some of the wealthier merchants— especially those who were members of the council— dressed in bright frilly clothes and wore gold around their necks and fingers. They were plump and always smelled of roast duck and venison.

While the wealthy lived fat lives, some men, women, and children lived on the streets. Daily they begged for bread and scraps. And a great many lived in homes that were so shabby that they offered little extra protection from the rain and cold than if they too lived on the streets.

Sister Wolf loved rich and poor alike but knew that she too was a beggar. She made sure to beg more often from the wealthy so that she could share with her poor brothers and sisters who struggled to survive.

As winter approached, the poor suffered. They didn't have thick, warm fur like Sister Wolf. Nor were they given as much food; Sister Wolf was treated as an honored guest, while the poor were ignored.

That winter was especially cold. The ground was frosty and the air chilly and damp. It was the sort of chill that cut through blankets and coats. It was a thick cold that soaked deep into bone.

The oldest person in the village, a wrinkly woman who smelled like onions, couldn't remember a winter so cruel.

"This is the worst winter of my life," she'd say. All agreed.

It was in that cruelest of winters that a band of outlaws began to attack nobles and merchants on the road from Stonebriar to nearby Brookhaven.

Many who left with gold rings around their fingers and gold chains around their necks returned with bare fingers and naked necks.

When these thefts happened, Sister Wolf didn't care. She didn't see much use for gold and jewels.

But then, one day, the outlaws killed a merchant on the road.

Sadness filled Sister Wolf. This merchant was a good man. He had a wife and three children. Sister Wolf let the youngest of the children, a gentle little girl with curly black hair who always giggled, ride on her back. When Sister Wolf came to the merchant's door, he didn't give scraps, but generous portions of whatever the merchant himself was eating.

Soon that sadness turned to anger. The anger turned to rage. Someone had murdered a member of her pack for meaningless pieces of shiny yellow rock.

During the night, instead of resting in her cave, Sister Wolf prowled the road to Brookhaven. She wanted to find the outlaws and kill them.

A man or woman would never have found them, but a wolf can find almost anything by scent. Before leaving Stonebriar, Sister Wolf had caught the scent of the outlaws from the clothes of the murdered merchant. The outlaws smelled the same as other humans, but they also smelled of cabbages.

They weren't hard for Sister Wolf to find. They were hidden far from the road, deep in the forest, in the ruins of a long forgotten chapel. There were five outlaws. They sat around a campfire. One was fat, one was thin, one was bald, one had long blond hair, and one wore an oddly pointy hat.

Sister Wolf waited in the shadows, listening. She had learned much of human speech from her time with the Beggar King. She was waiting for the best moment to attack.

As she waited, she overheard their conversation.

"I'm getting tired of cabbages," said the bald outlaw.

The skinny outlaw responded: "Then we shouldn't have robbed the cabbage merchant."

"Fair enough," replied the bald one.

The outlaw with the pointy hat took a bite out of a cabbage and said, "We can't keep living this way. We rob the nobles and the merchants, but what can we do with their gold? We can't enter a single village in the region for fear of arrest. It is getting cold and harder to hunt. And these ruins offer precious little protection from the cold and the rain!"

"We could turn ourselves in," said the very fat outlaw.

The skinny outlaw scowled. "That may have been an option when we were only guilty of poaching deer from the mayor's lands. We hunted to feed our families. But then we ran from the mayor's guards, which was an even greater crime. But now we're guilty of robbery . . . and murder," he grumbled.

The bald one agreed: "Even if we turned ourselves in, we'd surely hang."

The five outlaws quietly ate their cabbages. The one with long blond hair sniffled.

Feeling pity, Sister Wolf crept away.

That night, while the outlaws slept, she sneaked into to the camp and left a loaf of bread near the campfire. She did that night after night. Usually, she'd leave bread. Sometimes she would leave meat. It wasn't much; wolves can only carry with their mouths, but she hoped it would keep the men from attacking wealthy travelers on the road.

6

The School in the Forest

As winter set in, Stonebriar celebrated the twelve days of Christmas. Outside it was grey and cold, but the insides of homes and churches were brightly decorated and warm. During these days, the people of Stonebriar were especially generous, for Christmas was a time of sharing and love.

Sister Wolf and her fellow beggars received more food than usual. And not just bread and scraps! Sister Wolf ate smoked trout, candied pears, dried figs, and fresh baked bread. Sister Wolf was able to eat well during those days of abundance but still have plenty to share with the outlaws at night. She went to their camp each of the twelve nights of Christmas. Not once did the outlaws see her.

The outlaws had no idea who was bringing them food. The fat one thought it was a fairy or other forest spirit showing them kindness. The others all agreed that it was more likely to be a hermit. In those days, there were many hermits committed to simple lives of prayer throughout the countryside.

After Christmas came the worst of winter. The harsh bluster of January fell upon Stonebriar. Villagers gave Sister Wolf and the beggars less food. Rarely was there enough to share with the outlaws. And so, the outlaws once again started to attack travelers on the road to Brookhaven.

When Sister Wolf heard this, the heart in her furry chest sank. She understood their hunger but was committed to protecting the people of Stonebriar. Sister Wolf started traveling with the merchants and nobles along the road.

One day, while Sister Wolf was walking alongside one of the nobles, the outlaws attacked. Four of them brandished daggers while the skinny one carried a bow.

Leaping between the outlaws and the nobleman, Sister Wolf snarled and snapped her bared teeth. Since there was no longer violence in her heart, her ferocity was pretend. She hoped the outlaws would be scared enough to run away.

Sure enough, the men turned and ran. They had heard of gentle Sister Wolf, but they still remembered the terrifying stories of the Blood Wolf.

That night in her cave, Sister Wolf couldn't sleep. She considered both the people of Stonebriar and the outlaws to be part of her new pack.

She thought of the rich nobles and merchants; they had more than they needed. She thought of the poor in their hovels and the beggars on the streets who had too little. She thought of the outlaws, who were like the beggars but were too willing to kill to get what they wanted.

And she thought of her good friend, the Beggar King. She remembered what the Beggar King had taught her about how hard it was for people to share.

Since her heart and mind were too full to sleep, she went for a walk under the cool light of the full moon.

As she walked, she watched the trees gently swaying in the breeze. She heard the hoot of a barn owl as it flapped into the night. Sister Wolf thought to herself, "Owls are able to make nests to keep out the cold. Why couldn't the outlaws be like barn owls?"

She kept walking, slowly making her way down the mountain towards the road to Brookhaven. She saw a frightened hare hop across her path. Sister Wolf thought to herself, "Hares are able to eat roots and wild vegetables all year long. Why couldn't the outlaws be like hares?"

Suddenly, Sister Wolf had an idea. She would ask the creatures of the forest to share their wisdom with the outlaws. If the outlaws could no longer go back to their villages, perhaps they could learn to live happily in the forest.

At first, none of the animals of the forest would let Sister Wolf get close enough to them to talk. After all, most of the animals had relatives who had been eaten by wolves. But there are some animals wolves don't eat, and it was these that listened to Sister Wolf.

A porcupine was the first to agree to teach the outlaws. She would show them where to find roots and tubers that were good to eat.

Next, an old boar with long tusks agreed to show the outlaws where to find wild berries and fruits.

A pair of turtledoves agreed to show the outlaws where to find seeds and nuts that were good for eating.

Finally, Sister Wolf walked to nearby Mount Meer to talk to a brown bear that lived there. She agreed to teach the outlaws how to catch trout.

The porcupine, boar, turtledoves, and brown bear all agreed to meet at Sister Wolf's cave during the first sunrise after the new moon. In the meantime, Sister Wolf did her best to sneak food to the outlaws.

One day, as Sister Wolf begged for food, she caught the mingled scent of wheat and fire, willow and pine, raven and stone. It was the scent of her dear friend, the Beggar King! She ran to him, tail wagging and he gave her a big hug.

Joyfully, Sister Wolf told him of her plans. The Beggar King, who had learned to live comfortably in both city, field, and forest, agreed to teach the outlaws how to make shelters and clothing from whatever they could scavenge.

During the first sunrise after the new moon, Sister Wolf set out with her fellow teachers. They arrived at the outlaw camp just as the men were splitting a small rabbit for their meager breakfast.

When the porcupine, boar, brown bear, and wolf emerged from the bushes, the outlaws jumped to their feet in fear. When the Beggar King also stepped out of the bushes with a turtledove on each shoulder, their fear turned to wonder.

The Beggar King said, "Outlaws, we know you are hungry and cold. But you must no longer attack travelers on the road to Brookhaven. Sister Wolf, who cares for you so much that she's been sneaking you food for months, has come to teach you another way to live."

Overcome with gratitude for Sister Wolf's generosity, the outlaws were speechless. They remained silent for a time. When a beggar, a wolf, a bear, a porcupine, a boar, and two turtledoves ask you to do something, it is wise to listen.

So began the school of the forest.

The porcupine showed them where to find roots and tubers that were good for food.

The old boar taught them where to find wild berries and fruits.

The doves showed them how to find seeds and nuts.

The Beggar King taught them how to build simple shelters and how to use plant fibers (like milkweed) and bird feathers to make their clothes warmer.

The brown bear had the toughest job. She tried to teach the outlaws how to scoop trout out of the stream, but it was too cold for them. In the end, the outlaw with the oddly pointy hat was able to weave a simple net to catch fish instead.

The school in the forest continued well into spring. The animals and the Beggar King taught them everything they could. Eventually, the outlaws were able to care for themselves and even begin to store wild grains and nuts and seeds. They were able to dry edible roots and fish and berries.

It was a hard, but good life.

7

The Funeral

Midsummer approached.

The outlaws were able to build simple homes and storage huts amidst the ruins they called home. Soon, they were able to send word (by asking Sister Wolf to carry notes written on scraps of paper) for their families to join them.

The Beggar King visited from time to time. He taught them how to accept each day as it came, and not to worry about the future. The outlaws gave him all the gold they had stolen, which the Beggar King in turn gave to those in need.

The turtledoves decided to stay with the outlaws. The boar and the porcupine visited often. The bear went back to her home to start a family of her own.

Sister Wolf visited them most nights, but no longer needed to bring them food. In fact, sometimes the outlaws would share their food with her.

The outlaws were content.

Unfortunately, the outlaws hadn't been forgotten. For months, the village council had been sending soldiers to search for the outlaws. Each time the soldiers left Stonebriar, Sister Wolf followed at a distance.

One day, the soldiers discovered the outlaw camp. They were out on a routine search when they caught the scent of roasting vegetables. They followed their noses to the hidden camp. The outlaws were surprised. The captain, seizing the moment, yelled to his soldiers, "Draw your swords!"

At this, Sister Wolf leapt out from the shadows and stood between the soldiers and the outlaws. Whenever the captain took a step towards the outlaws, Sister Wolf drew closer to him. Instead of growling or snarling, Sister Wolf just looked him in the eyes, head low.

It was then that the outlaw with the oddly pointy hat spoke to the captain. "We surrender! We are guilty of robbery and even murder. Though we committed our crimes out of desperation and hunger, we have earned your punishment. Nevertheless, we ask for mercy."

Then the fat outlaw interrupted: "We promise to never harm anyone ever again! Sister Wolf brought a bear, a porcupine, a boar, two turtledoves, and the Beggar King to teach us how to live simply in the forest! We now live off of the land and even gave all the gold we stole to the poor!"

At this, the captain laughed. "You expect me to believe that?"

Then the captain saw two turtledoves resting on the shoulders of one of the outlaws' children. He saw a boar sleeping by the campfire and a porcupine scratching his nose near the feet of the skinny outlaw. And Sister Wolf, who was beloved by all of Stonebriar, stood quietly in front of him, looking him in the eye.

That day, the captain and his soldiers made a solemn promise to keep the outlaw camp a secret, so long as they promised to never trouble another traveler again. If a murderous wolf could change her ways, why couldn't a group of outlaws?

* * *

Seasons passed.

The soldiers kept their promise. The captain even visited the outlaws to help harvest food. In time, he left his post and joined the outlaw community.

The outlaw community was happy and healthy. Some seasons were harder than others, but even when their bellies were empty, their hearts were full. It was a joyous life. They were free to live in harmony with the forest without fear.

Sister Wolf traveled the countryside. Stories of her adventures spread; throughout the region, the people praised her compassion and courage. These stories have been passed down from generation to generation and are still told by bedsides and around campfires 'til this day.

As the seasons passed, her old injury began to bother her more and more. She had to put her adventuring days behind her. Nevertheless, she tried to visit the outlaws every Sunday, to join them for prayer and singing (Sister Wolf howled along).

Then, one day, she stopped visiting. Weeks passed. During an evening campfire, the Beggar King appeared and told them that Sister Wolf was very sick and didn't have much longer to live.

So it was that the five outlaws, in the dead of night, came to Sister Wolf's cave to say goodbye. The five of them, along with the Beggar King, were with her when she died. She died a happy wolf, surrounded by true friends.

At sunrise, the Beggar King carried the thin body of Sister Wolf to the gate of Stonebriar. When he got to

the city gate, he yelled up to the guard with the grey beard, "Open the gate!" And he did.

News spread quickly. The council decided to throw a lavish funeral. All of Stonebriar attended. Except, of course, Grumpus the rooster.

Some folks (and animals) don't believe people (or animals) can change. Grumpus never forgave Sister Wolf. Stubbornly, he stayed home.

And so, everyone (except Grumpus) crowded the streets as six city guards carried an ornate coffin containing the body of Sister Wolf to a gravesite near the center of the village.

Sparing no expense, the council built a small marble chapel over her grave. Above the marble altarpiece hung a gold-plated cross with precious gems. Sadly, the council wouldn't allow the beggars inside the chapel. The council members worried they'd get it dirty or try to sleep in it.

Every year, on the anniversary of Sister Wolf's death, Stonebriar would ring the chapel bell and the city would observe an hour of silence. Many visited the chapel to pray. But those who knew and loved Sister Wolf the best never set foot in the chapel.

The outlaws honored Sister Wolf differently.

They observed the anniversary of Sister Wolf's death by hosting a feast. Many of the animals of the forest joined them, as did some of the beggars from Stonebriar. In the outlaw community, all were welcomed as honored guests.

On that day, the Beggar King would pray outside the marble chapel in Stonebriar before heading to the feast at the outlaw camp.

Every year, they served nut cakes, smoked fish, roasted vegetables, fresh fruit, and hearty bread.

At the end of the evening, all would gather around a large campfire as the Beggar King shared the tales of Sister Wolf, including the one of how he met Sister Wolf. It is the story that you now know, beloved reader.

It is the story of a red wolf who was born to become the Lord of the Forest. She tried to rule through fear, but learned to serve with love.

The Legend of Francis
and the Wolf

A Wolf at the Gate is inspired by the legend of Saint Francis and the Wolf of Gubbio. In the legend, Francis (who I refer to in my story as "the Beggar King") is the hero, not the wolf. I've always wondered what the story would be like from the wolf's point of view.

Saint Francis is one of the most beloved people in history. Inspired by the life and message of Jesus, he lived in poverty, cared for the sick, and shared a story of God's love with people and animals alike.

Is the story true? Did Saint Francis meet a murderous wolf? Did that wolf turn from its violent ways and become friends with an entire village?

Here's what we know:

Francis lived in Gubbio around the year 1220. According to tradition, Gubbio gave the wolf an honorable burial and later built the Church of Saint Francis of the Peace at the site of the wolf's burial.

In 1872, during renovations of the Church of Saint Francis, workers discovered the skeleton of a wolf under a slab near the church wall.

The facts speak for themselves.

About Mark and Joel

Mark Van Steenwyk lives in a big old house in Minneapolis with his wife Amy, his son Jonas, and an assortment of friends. Their home is one of two houses of hospitality that share food and lodging with strangers. This is his first book for children. He's written a few other books to help grownups become more like the red wolf.

Joel Hedstrom is an illustrator working in the Twin Cities. He graduated in 2010 with a BFA from the College of Visual Arts. His influences include Japanese woodblock prints, tattoos, Greek vases, and printmaking.

Songs for *A Wolf at the Gate*

Jon Felton and his Soulmobile

CD • 30 minutes

$10.00

Jon Felton and his Soulmobile combine acoustic Appalachian instruments, punk energy, and a hint of silliness to illuminate the plot, themes, and characters of Mark Van Steenwyk's award-winning book for youngsters, *A Wolf at the Gate*. Humorous and singable, these may be the first songs about class struggle, income inequality, and creative nonviolence that your child loves. Good for grown-ups, too.

About Jon Felton and his Soulmobile:

It's like this: SOULMOBILE's always riding off into the dusty old horizon. That's their home. Fending off dangers untold with guitars, banjo, dulcimer, drums, and whatever's nearby, Camp Soul is holding out and ringing a bell. Jon carries the vision, the others hold him up and give the thing its shape. Body and soul, maybe: Properly difficult to distinguish. In any case, if you peek in on them don't be bashful; I think you'll find them welcoming to strangers.

ABOUT PM PRESS

PM Press was founded at the end of 2007 by a small collection of folks with decades of publishing, media, and organizing experience. PM Press co-conspirators have published and distributed hundreds of books, pamphlets, CDs, and DVDs. Members of PM have founded enduring book fairs, spearheaded victorious tenant organizing campaigns, and worked closely with bookstores, academic conferences, and even rock bands to deliver political and challenging ideas to all walks of life. We're old enough to know what we're doing and young enough to know what's at stake.

We seek to create radical and stimulating fiction and nonfiction books, pamphlets, T-shirts, visual and audio materials to entertain, educate, and inspire you. We aim to distribute these through every available channel with every available technology, whether that means you are seeing anarchist classics at our bookfair stalls; reading our latest vegan cookbook at the café; downloading geeky fiction e-books; or digging new music and timely videos from our website.

Contact us for direct ordering and questions about all PM Press releases, as well as manuscript submissions, review copy requests, foreign rights sales, author interviews, to book an author for an event, and to have PM Press attend your bookfair:

PM Press • PO Box 23912 • Oakland, CA 94623
510-658-3906 • info@pmpress.org
Buy books and stay on top of what we are doing at:
www.pmpress.org

 ## ABOUT REACH AND TEACH

Reach And Teach is a peace and social justice learning company, transforming the world through teachable moments. They publish and distribute books, music, posters, games, curriculum, and DVDs that focus on peacemaking and healing the planet.

Reach And Teach
144 W. 25th Ave.
San Mateo, CA 94403
www.reachandteach.com

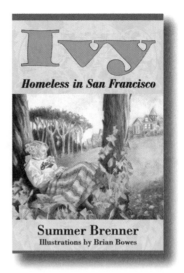
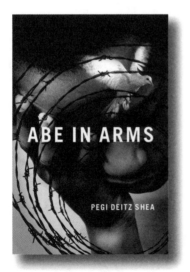

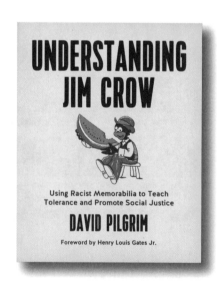
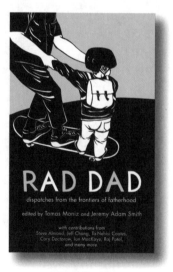